Kit Gets Peckish

Vivien Leanne Saunders

Kit Gets Peckish

Written and Illustrated by

Vivien Leanne Saunders

Once upon a time, there was a Bearded Dragon called Kit. He lived in a big, cosy house with a huge garden and a human who loved him very much.

Kit was not a clever lizard, but he was very curious.

One summer day he wriggled out of an unlocked window and ran into the garden. It was full of delicious salad, beautiful flowers and brightly coloured mushrooms.

Kit thought, "This garden is a magical place!"

Suddenly, Kit heard a high-pitched shriek. He looked up and saw a huge owl flying in the sky.

Birds eat Bearded Dragons!

Kit had been so excited he had wandered under the owl's nest by mistake.

He ran away as fast as he could, and hid until the owl flapped back to her nest.

Kit was not a very clever lizard.

All that running made Kit very hungry. He puffed out his beard and stalked through the long grass hunting for bugs to eat. He saw a dragonfly sipping dew off a grass stalk. It looked too pretty to eat!

"Are you a fairy?" Kit asked.

Dragonflies are honest little bugs. She started to shake her head. Before she could explain, Kit interrupted: "You look like a dragonfly, and dragonflies are delicious!"

"I'm a fairy." The dragonfly said quickly.

Kit was very disappointed. His stomach growled. The shiny bug really did look magical, though. He couldn't eat a fairy.

Kit was not a very clever lizard.

Kit trudged into the dark, damp mud to look for worms. He loved worms! He saw a big, fat spider dangling from her web. She had overheard the dragonfly's lie, and quickly ran up her silken thread.

"Don't eat me!" she shrieked, "I'm not a spider! I'm a witch! Look at how I spin magic in the air!"

Kit tilted his head and stared at her. His mouth watered. The spindly creature did look quite eerie. He didn't want a witch to curse him with an ugly face or bad breath!

"Sorry to bother you," he said politely, and left.

Kit was not a very clever lizard.

Kit waddled over to a patch of lettuce. He crunched up some lovely green leaves, but his tummy still felt empty. He saw a hairy caterpillar chewing on an apple.

The caterpillar was not a very good liar.

"Don't eat me!" he squeaked, "I'm a... erm... I'm a lion!"

Kit peered at the caterpillar. He didn't look like a lion. Lions were big, scary animals with bushy manes. The caterpillar did have a hairy mane, but he was tiny.

Kit remembered that he had once been a little lizard inside a small blue egg. Perhaps lions were tiny when they hatched!

He shivered and wondered if the caterpillar's grown-up mother would pounce on him the second he went *crunch!*

Kit was not a very clever lizard... ...but he knew something strange was going on. He pillowed his hungry head on his fat little beard, sighed, and thought:

The fairy fluttered like a dragonfly!

The witch was as spindly as a spider!

The lion was as wriggly as a worm!

Kit realised that all of them had lied to him!

He was furious! He turned around, already licking his lips, to hunt down the mischievous insects.

Kit forgot to watch the sky!

There was a horrible shriek, and the owl swooped down! She trapped poor little Kit in her massive claws.

"Don't eat me!" Kit squeaked.

He suddenly realised why all the bugs had played a trick on him. They didn't want to be eaten either!

He tried to lie, like they had, "I'm a dragon!"

She wasn't fooled for a second! Owls are very wise.

"YOU LOOK LIKE LUNCH TO ME!"

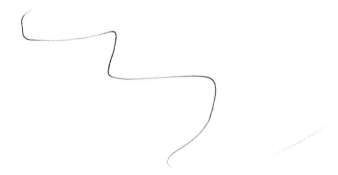

Kit closed his eyes.

The owl's sharp beak got closer...

...and closer...

...and closer...

...until...

"A GIANT! A GIANT!"

The owl flapped her wings and flew away, shrieking.

Kit looked up and saw a huge pair of hands reaching down. They picked him up, and the little Bearded Dragon felt himself being lifted high up into the sky.

"No, it's not a giant!" he shouted back at the owl, "It's my human!"

Now, Kit was not a very clever lizard....

But *this* time...

...he was right!

THE END

Bearded Dragon Facts

Not all Bearded Dragons are as stupid as Kit! But they can be very silly, so when we keep them as pets we have to know all about them. Here are some facts about nature's daftest, podgiest lizard:

1. They need to stay warm and cosy. They don't have any soft fur or feathers like cats or birds, so in the winter they can get very cold!

2. Yes, they *do* eat insects! In the wild they are very greedy and will eat whatever they can catch. When they're pets, they eat wriggly worms, chirping crickets and even bouncy grasshoppers! For

pudding they love fruit (especially blueberries), salad leaves and lots of yummy calcium dust to keep their bones strong.

3. When they get too hot, Bearded Dragons pant like dogs! Their tongues are very long and sticky, and their teeth are so small they're hard to see!

4. They come from Australia, where it's very hot and dry. A lot of Bearded Dragons don't drink water at all. They get all the water they need from their food.

5. Like plants, they need sunlight to grow! In rainy countries like England, their humans buy them special lightbulbs which they can bask under.

6. Their spikes are soft! They only get prickly when they're angry.

7. When they're *really* cross, they can change colour! They puff themselves out like a balloon and make their big beards black to scare off their enemies... or humans who annoy them.

8. Bearded Dragons have three eyes! The third one is on top of their head, so they can look straight up for birds. It looks like a freckle.

9. The oldest ever Bearded Dragon was Sebastian, who lived for 18 years! That's 126 in Bearded Dragon years!

10. It is risky for Bearded Dragons to be outside alone, so if you have a pet Bearded Dragon, make sure she or he always wears a leash outside, and keep an eye out for birds!

This book was inspired by my pet Bearded Dragon: Kit Kat Pancake. He was named that by my cousin, who saw him flattening out like a pancake!

Bearded Dragons do that to absorb as much light and heat as they can before the sun sets.

If you had a Bearded Dragon, what would you name it?

Cover design and Illustrations by Vivien Leanne Saunders
Based on the professional modelling skills of Kata Loki "Kit Kat Pancake Butt" Saunders
Edited by Vivien Leanne Saunders and humoured by George Glass

This book is a work of fiction. Names, characters, places, and incidents either are products of the author's imagination or are used fictitiously. Any resemblance to actual persons, living or dead, events, or locales is entirely coincidental.

Vivien Leanne Saunders
Visit my website at https://sivvusleanne.wixsite.com/authorvls

Printed by KDP Direct
First Printing: 2020
This Edition: 2020

Printed in Poland
by Amazon Fulfillment
Poland Sp. z o.o., Wrocław